MR.CHEERFUL

MR. CHEERFUL

by Roger Hargreaves

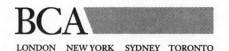

BCA

LONDON   NEW YORK   SYDNEY   TORONTO

Mr Cheerful always woke up in a
cheerful mood, with a bright
sunny smile on his face.

In fact Mr Cheerful was one of the most
cheerful people you are ever likely to meet.

He did, however, have one secret
that made him sad,
but nobody knew about it.

Not yet, anyway.

All I can tell you is that he liked to
keep it under his hat.

Mr Cheerful was never without a smile.

From breakfast time in the morning …

… to his bath time at night,
Mr Cheerful beamed from ear to ear.

He was even happy when it rained.

And on a sunny day,
his smile was even brighter and sunnier
than the sun.

Everybody around him couldn't help
but feel cheerful.

Even the flowers smiled when Mr Cheerful
walked past.

When Mr Funny met him, he felt so happy
that he pulled an even
funnier face than usual,
making Mr Cheerful laugh out loud.

Then one day, while out for a walk,
Mr Cheerful bumped into Little Miss Splendid.

Mr Cheerful smiled his usual cheerful smile.

Little Miss Splendid began to smile,
but then she stopped, and looked sternly
at Mr Cheerful.

"How rude!" she exclaimed. "Young man, don't you know that you should raise your hat when you meet a lady!"

For the first time in his life
Mr Cheerful lost his smile.

And then he blushed, bright red!

But he still did not raise his hat.

"You should be ashamed of yourself!"
cried Little Miss Splendid.
"Why won't you raise your hat?"

"I'm too embarrassed," replied Mr Cheerful,
blushing an even brighter red.
"Without my hat on I'm not very good-looking
and that makes me sad."

"Really?" asked Little Miss Splendid.
"Let me see."

Mr Cheerful lifted his hat.

And now I'll tell you what his secret was.

Mr Cheerful had the grand total
of only three hairs on his head!

"Is that all you're worried about?"
asked Little Miss Splendid.
"Why, it's your bright sunny smile
that everybody loves, not how many hairs
you have on your head!"

And Little Miss Splendid smiled.

Then Mr Cheerful smiled.

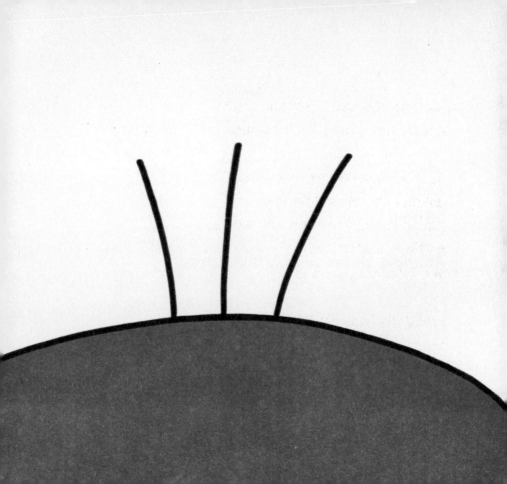

And ever since that day
he hasn't stopped smiling.

And he is always quick to raise his hat
to everyone he meets.

And everyone he meets goes away
feeling happy and cheerful.

Which leaves only one thing
left to say …

… hats off to Mr Cheerful!